WE ARE MAKING THE WORLD A BETTER PLACE

K.I. HOPE

WE ARE MAKING THE WORLD A BETTER PLACE

Printed in the United States of America

First Edition

ISBN: 978-0-9968064-0-4

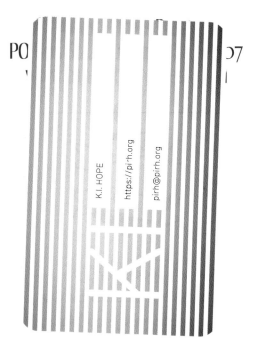

1010 1001 1000 111 110 101 100 11 10 1

for Øivar

I couldn't tell you why the noodles, set on the red-rimmed white plate before me, became worms. If I could better explain perspective, I wouldn't bother with this narration. But there they sat, the Shanghai noodles, my former favorite, suddenly ridged and writhing, trying to shake the sauce, feeling themselves slick with hoisin, undulating towards some greater invertebrate good unbeknownst to, and away from, me. I reached for my tea, careful to not let my sleeve get too close, and watched them, just a pile of worms, upset by the chunks of dead cow they were sharing space with on this generic, vaguely-Asian plate.

They didn't stop moving even when the server came by to nod in my general direction and point at the untouched food. I ate this meal at least twice a week. I ate it with abandon, and quickly, checking the time and messages on my phone throughout. Today, the teacup barely left my lips and the noodles just sat. I shrugged to him, and he walked off, returning with the bill and a teapot I declined. I put my card down on the check and reached for the chopsticks, thinking that worms are not that unusual of a food in some parts of the world - maybe the issue was with me. Who was I to place my cultural standards of what is considered edible over those of another?

I brace myself and watch as the chopsticks slowly move down. The cheap sticks of splintering wood begin their approach, and the worms seem to move faster, as if they know a predator is near. But worms don't feel fear, do they? I remember as a child, chopping one in half and watching both sides continue with life, which makes me more uneasy about their journey inside my stomach.

Cautiously, I trap one with the chopsticks and place it in my mouth. It squirms inside, so I start chewing, hoping to bite down on something that will stop the motion that is not my tongue, since the textures are so similar. It seems to work, and there is a warm gush of liquid, a sour note, mingling with the oyster sauce and ginger and burnt sugar, that becomes a different taste entirely. I masticate as best I can, and feeling my stomach growl, continue.

I make it through about a third of the plate

before the pinging of my phone can no longer be ignored. I check my watch and see the sync of messages flowing, little cascading demands, all of which must be met immediately, and in the office.

As I stand to leave, the owner walks up to me and pats me on the back.

"Why didn't you order your usual?"

"What?"

"You asked for the house specialty instead, so I brought it, but I didn't really think you'd even try it. Good for you."

"I ..." I didn't remember doing this. "I wanted to step outside of my comfort zone."

He laughs, nodding like this is not the first time he's heard someone like me say something like that. "Congratulations." He bows, and then shakes his head.

"Next time, get the damn noodles."

That night my stomach feels like tapeworms are destroying it, but I try to reason with myself and say it's only my imagination. I search online for information on eating worms but most of the results talk about the kind of worms you get from eating raw meat, not from eating the worms themselves. Did it happen? Was it a joke? A nice reprieve in what I am sure is a disconcertingly predictable routine?

Another attempt to eradicate my painful whiteness? I await the coming of the cream that will tint my skin enough to show I am not as insensitive as my appearance suggests.

But though the medicine cabinet holds no such miracles, it does have a nice display of pills to alleviate all modern maladies, though there isn't one conspicuously for cross-cultural culinary mishaps. A mix of digestive enzymes and painkillers, then, and a green juice in the morning, will cure what ails without fail.

The couch is still home to yesterday's arguments, as the blankets stayed in the nest formation I made as I feigned sleep while wanting forgiveness, and since the bedroom door is closed, I return to fighting with the cushions instead of her, saving her stale morning breath for fresh lungs.

The coffee machine clicks on a few hours later. It commences the start of its very short, ten-minute work day with three loud beeps, which will also sound again at the end to announce the arrival of eight-to-ten cups of freshly brewed coffee, the amount depending on if it's a weekday or weekend. I am jealous of the coffee machine's schedule. Of it only needing to serve one function and still be allowed to occupy space in this world. Of my girlfriend's hands touching it before me every morning. But as much as we are all dependent on caffeine in our civilization, our civilization is far more dependent on people like me than that particular kind of machine.

I hear the carafe being pulled from the spout, a little plastic click as it releases, and I know she is awake and standing in the kitchen. I know that she is about thirty minutes away from leaving the apartment. I know that she is so focused on her work day that has yet to begin (or maybe she always brings it home with her, sleeping with it more than me) she will not notice or care if I am awake or asleep on the couch. So I pretend to sleep, I wait it out. I take advantage of the culture of my job that I don't have to wear a suit to show up. I pull the blanket over my face and scroll through my watch, ensuring there are no immediate needs to be met, holding my urine, listening to the hairdryer, waiting for the bathroom to empty.

The door closing is a starting gunshot, and I am showered and dressed and standing at the bus stop in fifteen minutes. The morning is gray; it is summer. I stare at the coffee shop across the street and think of a cortado and that thick cinnamon toast and coconut water, but know if I can hold out until I arrive at work it will be free, and so I must, since sixty percent of my salary goes to rent and another thirty to student loans. I shift on my feet, my bag slung over my shoulders, windbreaker open and lying haphazardly underneath the strap. The bus stop starts to swell with bodies, they come from every corner of these streets, crawling through the cracks, seemingly rising from the gutters, as bathed in filth as the hills are in fog. I back up against the glass and keep my eyes averted; be a stranger, all the time.

No one speaks. They just sway to some song that is the soundtrack of survival, a dull heartbeat, erratic and arrhythmic, making for offbeat dancing, awkward living. I try to keep mine steady, alternating taps of my toes, slowly, so as not to call attention to myself. A man pulls a hand-rolled cigarette from his pocket, tobacco flaking out onto the concrete. The scent fills my nostrils, filters down into my lungs, but I refuse to cough. I don't want him to see me. I don't know what the world looks like through his eyes, but I imagine there is such a filter of remove ignoring me is easy. A few more minutes and they'll all be gone.

The city bus pulls up when he's halfway done smoking, and he pools saliva on his tongue and puts it out, saving it for the next stop. The driver doesn't even bother to hold the doors for me anymore, they've all adjusted. The bus shudders and starts up again, the accordion in its center sighing out its sad tune. When it passes I can see across the street again, and my thoughts turn back to those little luxuries that I fight with myself about constantly. I think of my girlfriend and how she probably stopped there after leaving the house, waited for the car to come and gather her, and how we've never had coffee there together on a workday. Only the weekends, and even then, it's usually somewhere else for brunch.

Next door the old Italian restaurant sits closed, butcher paper pasted to the windows, a poem resting on the door. I hear a large clothing company has already purchased the space, and protests are starting against the gentrification. Part of the charm of this area is the multiculturalism, and plenty of the new residents strive to preserve it against all odds.

The white bus arrives a moment later and I climb on and head to my normal seat, two thirds back on the left side. As I am swinging my messenger bag over my head, my watch vibrates, alerting me that the bus is approaching. They need to fix this - it's been this way for months since the latest update. I used to wait inside my apartment for the notification, but after missing the last shuttle to work a few times I started coming downstairs early, which means being caught in the regular traffic, being a part of the heartbeat of the city, and feeling about as valuable as plaque in the arteries.

That changes though once I am among my coworkers. A few nod, but many have already started their work day and don't notice new passengers, their tablets displaying a stream of data they furiously catalog. Rather than working with algorithms, my job consists of working with words.

I am not a writer, despite for a time fantasizing about writing long accounts of my own journeys in far-flung locations across the globe, giving a voice to the experiences of people everywhere, uniting us all by illuminating the common struggles we endure. The words I see today, and every day, filling the screen of my tablet, are the words of those people directly. No longer in need of a cartographer to map out their pain, people now go online to scream their frustrations, and I am there to clean and bandage their wounds and ensure they don't cut each other too deeply.

That is, in essence, my employ. I know my girlfriend doesn't see it as being as difficult as her work, but I do. I know my coworkers, the architects, don't see it as an essential support of the information skyscrapers they build. I see it as a fulfillment of that childhood dream, of storytelling, of sharing our human experience. In a way that facilitates conversation, connection, between everyone, regardless of ⸗

The shuttle lurches and comes to a fast stop. We are approaching the entrance to the freeway. Cars sit, waiting for the metered light to allow them to merge. Pull up to the line, wait for the green, maybe jump it and save yourself a few seconds. Seconds. We live in a time when time is measured in seconds. I wonder what those in history felt when a day would pass. They had eaten, maybe, if they were lucky. They would sleep, hard. There was day, and night, work and rest. We live by seconds. Seconds it takes for information to transmit through cables, at the bottom of oceans, wrapping around the Earth five times: financial data sails below the currents from Hong Kong to New York. New ones are installed to save *split*-seconds, giant leviathans curling underneath the depths, carrying the currencies of world economies through its stomach. Evolution, everything, all of it, is going faster, faster, *faster...*

But us. We sit. We stare at screens.

I break the connection and glance out the tinted windows of the shuttle. Cars line the lanes in both directions, unmoving. I can make out a few faces of frustration, a woman applying mascara in the rearview, many mouths talking animatedly with peripherals in their ears. I can't help but hear the voices of politicians, arguing about high speed rail and electric cars and advancements costing too much money, voters unable to make up their minds. If only they would all just get out of the way, all of them. They don't understand what we are trying to accomplish *for them*, to remove all of these obstacles of daily life. Highways shouldn't look like cemeteries for cars with bouquets of fossil fuels resting on top of each tombstone. There are better alternatives. We will make them.

Maybe you don't think any of this is important. Maybe I am not convincing you. Perhaps your heart is older, longing for a simpler time. Perhaps your heart is young, and unbreakable. Mine, it has survived the quarter-life crisis, it has adapted, it has progressed. Progress. That is what we are talking about, isn't it? That is the zeitgeist of my time. No longer bound to the slow churn of the mill, so far from dragging blocks to build pyramids. And beyond infrastructure, we are building the most important element of all human civilization: tolerance. There is a kinder, gentler world coming. The revolution will be homogenized.

10

I feel lost within their laughter, smaller still sitting in this restaurant, shrinking into my seat. The back of the seat is straight, the space is sparse, modern, done only in muted tones with bamboo plants, the music is electronic, the food is deconstructed. It is a booth, it is plush, it is a speakeasy throwback, it is kitsch, candlelight, the music is remixed classics, the food is comforting. I balance on a barstool made of reclaimed wood at a communal table with mason jars for glasses, the chefs have tattoos, the music is acoustic, the food is hyperlocal. It is all of those places, and none of them, it is a repetition and a redundancy and an obligation I dread.

My girlfriend's firm is always throwing

these dinners for the partners and the rotating door of their favorite associates, of which she is a perennial. I watch the other faces change from meal to meal, coming and going as fast as food trends and famous chefs in this city. But hers, that placid, still face, like a lake set in the center of a mountain no man can reach, save seeing it a thousand miles away by airplane, is the centerpiece to each night.

From that first summer she clerked her value was clear, cut brilliant like the kind of diamond I will never be able to afford that sits on other womens' hands, weighing them down, making them drag their knuckles across tablecloths as they reach for the dessert fork like dressed-up neanderthals, the only kind of homo sapien left alive today that surely must not see the blood tinting the carbon. But those women are her bosses, and they expect better for her than I can give.

I have heard her asked why she is with me. *He is so passiona*te, is always her answer. *He believes in the greater good.* I am a preacher, it seems, of social justice and equality; the karma I collect to one day pay her debts.

So I don't always attend these evenings. They eat late constantly, and drink brown spirits neat or with orange peels and bitters, sometimes a cherry sunken to the conical bottom of the glass, resting above the stem. I see her fingers run the length of it, like she is always contemplating each sip before she brings it to her lips. Like every breath that leaves her body is a calculation of what she can expel and what she needs to recover that loss.

No matter what seat I take or what shape the table, I am always away from her.

The key clicks in the lock and I push, the door is heavy but moves effortlessly with the help of a hydraulic hinge. It closes resolutely behind us, quietly, sealing us in our domesticity, segregated from the outside world, from other couples whose lives we may seek to emulate should we observe them too much. There is an appropriate amount of comparison and reflection before it edges into obsession with a second life that will never exist. But, she likes to talk about the neighbors; this building is lousy with young love.

She goes straight to the kitchen and pours herself wine. She knows I don't want any. I lost count of her drinks at dinner but I swear her stomach is made of a salt that covers all the fire of alcohol. Or maybe her soul is a pillar, as erect as her spine, as she steadfastly stares into her immoral past and our questionable relationship. Sometimes I think the drinking is so that she can focus on a different kind of nausea, the sickness of saturation, instead of the revulsion she feels from my hands on her skin.

To hear her tell it, we are perfectly

complementary, the heart and the brain, together animating a body that forever marches into a glorious sunrise, wherein the world will recognize us and cast us in bronze in a center square, our faces tilted towards a future free of conflict, our hands carrying the borders that once stood between countries we tore down, coalescing us into global citizens.

I stand unsure, as unsure as I sat all through dinner, in our kitchen, or is it hers? I wait to see where the wine will take her, if it will touch her hand and pull her towards the bathroom for a solitary shower, or trip her as she undresses and sends her straight into bed. But she waits by the wineglass, looking down into the garnet-hued lagoon, swirling it and watching the tears stream down the glass with her dry eyes. I can't remember the last time I saw her cry.

She is in bed after a fumbled fucking in the living room. I close my eyes but see flashes of moments from it: her difficulty in unfastening my belt, her head lolling back on the arm of the couch as I watch her tits undulate in her bra that she often leaves on, the semen inside the condom I tie and throw in the trash next to the compost bin, where it rests in the interim before the era of biodegradable prophylactics arrives. I know that making love tastes like tannins for her, a sour note she can't quite clear, but craves anyway. For me the flavor is burnt, a beautiful piece of life taken and turned to death and then further destroyed by improper technique and carelessness. But it is filling nonetheless, it is nourishment, it is necessary. Just once, though, I wish to experience perfection, a masterful touch, a symphony of sensation, a moment of discovery that will forever alter the course of my life, or end it entirely.

But I am being maudlin, no? I am feeling sorry for myself, lamenting what I have, which is so much more than nearly everyone alive. I should not want for anything from my vantage, caressing the underside of the one percent, living a dozen floors below the penthouse, but still miles above the gutters, breathing in rarefied air, redolent of a city without filth. And yet I do, I do want for what I lack, and I try to take comfort in telling myself it is only human, but in a world so unconcerned with the humane it is of little comfort. I think of the people that step over the half-dead bodies littering the alleyways and ask themselves as they pass: *Why don't they change their situation?* And in the center of nights like this, I look at myself laying half-dead in the dark, reflected off the windowpanes, and ask myself the same.

The sun slips between the cables of the

bridge, casting long thin lines onto the bay, setting the water alight with a rose hue. On the hills sit tiny houses, illuminated by streetlamps that have not yet shut off for the day. The first few cars are gathering on the roadways below, but they sail along effortlessly, unencumbered by the traffic that has yet to collect. This morning is beautiful, and in the dawning of it I realize the somber thoughts of last night seem silly. It is like I am suddenly sober from my sadness intoxication, having slept off its effects to wake up with a headache stemming from shame, the guilt of comparing myself to those on the streets, the embarrassment of a night passing wherein I was unable to manage my emotions.

As that thought leaves me, the relief is replaced with anxiety about seeing her this morning; I do not want her to spoil my calm. I decide to leave before the coffee machine starts its cycle and go to the cafe across the street, to indulge in a luxury I typically am denied and catch the early shuttle into work. Tonight, whatever strangeness exists between us, it will not owe to my mood. I grab my things and head out the door, looking forward to living this exact day.

〉〉

After twenty minutes of standing in line it is almost my turn. I hear the woman in front of me asking for an espresso with a small amount of milk, and debating the nomenclature and origins of the drink with the barista.

"It's called a *cortado*, from the Spanish *cortar*: to cut."

"Actually, here it's known a Gibraltar, owing to the distinctive glassware." The barista smiles, and points above her to the menu, where, in clean font, *gibraltar* is nestled between con panna and cubano. She then extends her smile, showing full teeth, as if this will somehow make the correction more palatable.

"Well on the East Coast, it's a cortado," the woman sniffs, hoisting her calfskin purse back over her shoulder, nearly colliding with me as she turns to leave the register and wait for her drink.

I try to appear sympathetic when I move up in the queue, wanting the barista to know I am on her side, that she can relax when she speaks to me.

"Someone should really make a periodic table of coffee drinks," I say. She looks at me without expression, as flat as the foam on the Gibraltar another barista is making, the surface tension pulling it perfectly across the arch-cut squat glass.

"Someone has," she replies, and waits.

"Um," I stumble. "I'll have a twelve ounce ... what single-origins East African beans do you have right now?"

"The Tadiyass from Ethiopia," she replies without hesitation. "It has a nice chocolate tone underneath, highlighted by citrus and floral notes and a sweet, syrupy finish."

"Wow, uh, okay, that, please; and a piece of toast."

Her fingers move quickly over the touchscreen register.

"$12.50."

I keep my face blank so as not to react to the cost and hand her a credit card. It is one of those unspoken societal rules, never to balk at a price; it betrays too much weakness. She looks at my name on it and types in the first to call out for my order, and thanks me by saying my last.

She points to my watch as she hands my card back.

"We'll be upgrading our computer system soon to accept that method of payment. Sorry we're so out of date here."

"Oh... it's no problem. I mean, I just have this for work," I offer as a way of apology, not wanting to make *her* apologize for her employer's anachronous business practices. She has no control over it, surely, and it must be awful each time she has to refuse that option to customers that will inevitably wonder why they bother coming somewhere that cares so little to cater to their needs. I think of the ones that do blame her and feel sick.

She nods in acceptance and looks past me to the person next in line. By the time I walk over to the bar, the woman from the East Coast is already sitting on a stool, sipping her coffee, searching the room for some sign of what she left behind, what she was used to. I see that look all the time.

I gather my order and consume it slowly, knowing I have thirty minutes before the shuttle arrives, and I would rather wait in here than outside. I glance back on occasion to the register but the girl was replaced by someone else; I assume she is on break, maybe smoking in the alleyway, if that is still something young people that work in coffee shops do.

I finish my breakfast and walk to the compost and dish station to clear my mess, when the girl from the register appears, wiping down the condiment bar with a wet rag. I try to think of something to ask her, to keep her here for a moment with me, something no one else ever has asked, that will give her pause and perhaps even alleviate some dark secret she is keeping locked inside.

"What do you want from life?" I wince, hoping she does not recognize a frequent personal development question from our staff meetings. No, how could she? It is a general thing as well, something we all ask ourselves and others.

She considers it, I mean really considers it, like she wants to give me a deserving answer, a real human exchange instead of a standard line. God, she is beautiful.

"I don't know, I just don't want to work very hard." She shrugs. "But it's unfortunate, what's happening, that we are supposed to be delighted with doing more and more for less and less, and to say that we want to do less so that we may have more *time* is such an offensive thing, that to just exist is thought of as the most vile pursuit we are capable of." She looks at my watch again. "Yet this cafe is full of those able to enjoy leisure time."

I am startled by, and endeared to, her honesty. I am sympathetic to the sentiment she expresses, it is common among the locals of this city, though that breed seems to be dying out. Perhaps that is it, then, what she is describing: the desire to stay the same. It is an affliction suffered by so many.

"Don't you ever want to make something?"

"I make... coffee."

"No, I mean, something lasting."

She waves her hand around to the packed cafe. "I'd say this is an enduring cultural trend."

"No, I mean, something *important*," I hear myself saying before I have a chance to think about it. I am disgusted with the lack of editorial decisions I've made in this conversation.

She pauses, calculating far better than I have so far. I then come to understand, in her silence, in her hesitation, that she is at work, and I am not, and that mere inequity has forced her to trim her speech with much larger shears than I do mine.

"You must be terrible with women."

"I've got a girlfriend."

"You must be terrible with women."

I stand there, wondering how a person of such intellect and beauty can say she is satisfied at this coffee shop, arguing with customers about things like glasses and pointing out deficiencies the in men that talk to her. Surely she must want to use all of that for *something*, there must be a larger goal, a long-term plan, hiding, kept tucked away. Perhaps it is too fragile and she is afraid of clumsy hands dropping and breaking it: it has happened in the past. It was words, I am sure, that killed that dream, stabbed the little lion through the heart, poached it away from her and left her hot and barren and dry in the waterless wild. It is always words, the wrong ones, that cause carnage. It may be too late for her, but I think as I always do, of the child not yet stripped of ambition by those that would seek to deny others what they never had, and how I can stop them from harming her.

11

three

I don't know if I've taken enough time to talk to you yet. Things have been hectic, but they always are. It's not an excuse. I feel like you have seen some sides to me that you may find sharp, edges you don't want to run up against. In trying to think of how to best convey what it is that I feel, it is, as always, the beginning that seems an appropriate place to start. An interlude, then, a raft floating in the sea of routine. Let us rest awhile.

I find myself thinking back to notes passed in class in elementary school. Those little missives, scratched in childhood scrawl, contained endless possibilities of mystery. The anticipation when, in your peripheral, you caught the folded white square, light blue pinstripes running through, the impression of the ink inside visible from where a child's hand pressed hard on the page. And then came the brush pass: you took it and squeezed it between your legs, staring straight ahead, waiting to see if the teacher was aware of the covert communication, thinking desperately of what could be inside, each second that passed a century of agony.

Opening the note was enveloping, your vision confined to the letter, the other children in their seats disappearing, the once great fear of the pedagogical threat suddenly insignificant. And its contents could cause your heart to swell or burst, to become closer to a friend, or torn forever apart.

Worse still, than the note containing a little death, is if it was intercepted, confiscated, or disseminated, never to be read. Once it passed from your hand so too did the control. No longer was it between sender and recipient; there became an *other*, capable of ruination. So what then was the solution? Codes. *Symbols.*

You invented a language all your own, discarding the one of your native tongue, creating ideograms translated by a key comprised of inside jokes and shared interest; you made little words only the two of you could sound out. And what did you make them from? Nothing more than straight lines and circles, these symbols, the means to consign the very essence of your being. For what is any glyph distilled to but one long line? A fingertip, pressed and poised, pulling straight down, that is the beginning of everything.

Maybe it reeks of hubris, but sometimes when I think of what humans have built from the very symbols we created, it is like they all represented more than an idea, but a new god, a new omnipotent creature aiding and pacifying our turbulent lives. With our own symbols we were able to better invent gods suited to our modern needs. And conversely, reflecting on the destruction symbols can cause is like watching devils birthed inside souls.

What do I mean? What am I saying? I am saying that it was the animation of *symbols*, not machinery, that began the transcendence from individual cogs to collective consciousness.

Without the symbols, the machines humans first made are self-contained. The wheel continues rolling, the mill grinding, the clock ticking, but they stand autonomous, unable to link or communicate. For centuries, machines were little more than complicated tools. The printing press was a large pen. Furnaces burning in factories were large fires. Each stood on its own, waiting for man to come and give it life, to stir the coals, to use their own energy to stimulate the machines. But the symbols, they are able to move through wires as electricity, or across airwaves like breath. Once symbols were injected into machines, once raw materials taken from the earth were joined with the symbols expressed by the imagination and heart of man, only *then* did we arrive where we are now, in a time when we write our gospels in Python and bind our sacred books in binary.

I mean, think of it: what is ultimately nothing more than little lines and circles contains the entirety of not only human knowledge, but the entirety of human *emotion*. And those feelings are transmitted across the world instantly. People fall in love because of this. Babies are born because of this. Our world is no longer limited by latitudes. We traverse the most treacherous of topography over T1 lines. We are able to translate all of our distinct languages into the same: one that is understood by computers and then translated with more symbols, then into different ones understood by another person, and all in permanence, all in posterity.

It's alchemy, modern magic - the natural evolution of our ancestors drawing the animal they were to kill in the ground before the hunt; or early isolated cultures creating symbols with the same meanings independently of each other. These miracles may not look like what was prophesied, there are no plagues or floods or beasts to mark the end of ignorance and welcome salvation, but glowing screens, bathed holy in their light.

You think me a zealot, no doubt. We are all a little too devoted to that which we believe in. Even the staunch atheist believes steadfastly in his nonbelief. It is the medicine of the affliction of cognition to have faith. Faith not need be of a sect to have the necessary effect. You may think yourself without, that you are beyond needing such things, but I only ask to widen your definition, to see what it is in life you consecrate yourself to.

If you do answer that, then understand it is universal. That is all I am trying to say. We all have *something*. And we are at an unprecedented point where the sharing of our somethings is possible for everyone. I see beyond barriers, I understand the joining of hands we are doing, the world we are creating. We are all just students passing notes in a global classroom.

And I read those classroom notes. I am the teacher. I am the threat. But like the teacher of our youth, I mean no harm. I simply need to see what it says inside that folded piece of paper. When you were a child, you resented the teacher, thought him or her stupid; as an adult, you come to see the need for protection of our youth.

What if it is a threat of imminent harm, a cause to incite? Our very constitution deems that speech illegal. Same with slander or libel - you cannot maliciously defame another with lies. Or what of that most difficult one, *obscenity*, a vast word, spreading like a sickness as we are exposed to the darkest corners of the human mind. If we apply contemporary community standards, you will find there are things on the internet no one should see.

So do you object? Do you decry me a censor?

Or do you see me as an arbiter of standards, decided upon by consensus? After all, it is your comments I respond to, that of the community; it is sentiments that are widely accepted that remain, with only fringe elements dismissed after their inferiority is determined by the populous. In the marketplace of ideas I am just the broker. You are the lenders and borrowers; you set the terms of sale. *You* create the zeitgeist, I merely hold the mirror.

Does this still disturb? This group think? This silencing of dissent? I ask you, think further. Think beyond mere offenses or tears. What of the potential to save or take a life? You may scoff but think of the messages we have read only after it is too late: children slitting their wrists because of words. It seems to me these symbols have immense power. Like the ancient hunter would draw his prey in the dirt to guarantee a kill, so too does the bully. But the strokes are made upon keys, and the so-called predator sits behind the safety of the screen. So we return to the ways of vigilantes, not because our town sheriff is corrupt, he is just on the wrong side of the digital divide. In the chaos of the internet there must be a force to counteract these criminals.

There will always be those that seek to subvert. Those that say there is no need or no right to read those notes. The inventors of code. The protectors of privacy. That we must operate under the assumption of human goodness. That even if you have nothing to hide, you have the right to hide it. But what has this new world taught us if not the blackest side to our souls? We have all stumbled upon things we cannot clear from our cerebral caches. And there exists bleaker interests still, beyond your searches, for they are encrypted, unable to be accessed unless you have good reason to and pay good money, the market for which is large enough to fuel organized crime, an endless stream of victims fresh on the screen. Surprising? Who is to be held responsible for the theft of innocence from those children? Do you not think *this* the purview of an enforcer?

Then there are the spillers of secrets, who do so under the guise of the greater good, garnering public support and sympathy, for it is a sight to behold, the epic battle of handsome David against the governmental Goliath. People do not like to think they need governing, and these martyrs galvanize against surveillance - just that word, I am sure, sends cold chills down your spine. But have I taught you nothing thus far? Have you never seen the horrors firsthand? I do not wish to make a drought of an Arab spring, I do not want us to become a so-called "people's republic" where a search results in finite hits instead of the infinite. I only want to eat those who think themselves at the top of the food chain, to be the virus that kills what man cannot. I operate in reality, dear reader. All I ask is you do the same.

Maybe you have not seen enough. After all, if I am doing my job, that darkness is hid from the light of your screen. If the gatekeepers are trustworthy, then all who are trustworthy in return may enter the kingdom of knowledge. It is why it is essential the teacher remain in possession of notes, not to censor, but to *save*.

Perhaps though, still, this treatise is antithetical to that for which you stand. But there are many that take refuge in my work. They do not want to hear what the man next to them on the bus thinks of doing to their genitals. Or their children's. They do not wish to be wrongly accused of racism and lose their job; yet still want to ensure those holding tightly to antiquated ideas are held accountable. The culling of the collective consciousness requires a deft hand that does less than it does more. It is skimming the fat that collects at the top, leaving the bulk of everything to boil together in the soup pot. That film, that filth, the impurities, I remove it so that what is left is clarified, it is refined. And if it is not to be removed, then I create an emulsion, I make that which is by nature immiscible into a single, cohesive mixture, and I stand vigilant to make sure it does not break and separate. The entirety of human consciousness made homogeneous. I am writing the first movement of the symphony of the future, a sonata to welcome singularity, and while to you in this moment it may sound sharp or flat, there will come a time when it is sung proudly as the anthem by a united race.

I am keeping you safe. I am bringing you

closer to those you thought different. I am easing your burdens. I am making the world a better place.

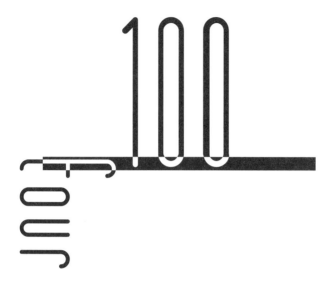

one hundred

four

The water comes in hard on the concrete, pushing the gray further up as it stains it with waves of rust. Beyond the bay walls sit barrels, biohazard warnings peeling off and flaking away into dust. The remains of a playground stand charred, a monument to childhoods lost, ash coating the ground where bark should be, the smell of melted plastic thick in the air, another toxin composing the compounds of the atmosphere here. I presume a funeral procession will pass, attendees dressed in white, burying one of the many taken before their time. I was once told that funerals are the main social event on Sundays in this neighborhood. I expect to hear gunshots.

There is only one road into this part of town, and hardly anyone born here ever makes it out. How could they, with just that straight line to walk? The strip of street, only recently outfitted with lightrail running through the center, has liquor stores galore and little more to serve those on the outer edge of the innermost chamber of the city, who wait to die young, isolated from one of the greatest cultural centers in the world.

Coming in you feel the shift. You watch as garbage collects in gutters, as bars appear on store windows, as more of those stores sit closed. The skin gets darker and you become painfully aware of the color of yours for the first time in your life. Once you cross the narrow bridge over the polluted water, the place you thought you called home ceases to exist. You become a visitor in another land, a tourist in your own town, feeling about as awkward as you do when you're forced to look at the old couples that swarm downtown in tacky shirts in the summer, obvious targets for ridicule.

Once inside, this parcel itself is prime, a developer's wet dream. It's on the waterfront, with views of the skyline, the bridges, a more temperate climate: a space to spread urban sprawl like a sickness. And they *are* developing, they will make it clean, they will make it lush and green. But we are at the coastline, we are below sea level, we are on the last barren piece of land in existence, needing to squeeze another twenty thousand people onto this square mile. For they are arriving with their carpetbags as they always have, as I did. But what about those that have lived here for generations? Where do they go when they get pushed out, into the ocean to drown? Do they watch the lights of the buildings and bridges glint like stars as they slip underneath the black water, sinking just out of reach of the city that never taught them to swim?

The city had decades to do so, though. But the blight sat, even after the federal government designated it a priority, even after taxpayers and industry alike dumped funds to the restoration of the wetlands. The ingrained segregation meant a lack of sympathy, meant the residents could fade into the night, for their plight was theirs and theirs alone. That love of the familiar, even when it is wrong, is a stubborn thing to scrub out. But now *we* have arrived, and erase it we will.

I watch my girlfriend from the window of the driver's seat. It is her car - I can't afford one - but I drive it; she is frightened of driving in the city. She slaughters those in the stands in the courtroom, but ask her to navigate hills and one way streets and traffic, and she panics. I see her standing with men dressed even better than her. I know the brands they wear from the cut of fabric, the tiny details, the off-color cuffs, the contrasts. She shifts her weight as they talk, knowing her shoes do not provide the kind of protection she would like from the pollutants of this place. Off to the side stands a government employee, required by law to be there but not included in the conversation. They will decide things, and then tell him. He will nod, file a report, collect a paycheck and wait for a pension. My girlfriend and these men, they will receive bonuses. Stock options. They, they are thoroughly incentivized. He is not.

What the government could not accomplish here in twenty-five years we will have done in less than three. I have seen the artist's rendering, the open spaces, the units set aside for below-market-rate housing, the university satellite campus that will focus on bringing science, math and technology to this historically underserved area, closing the gap on the digital divide. There will be diversity, a new wave of immigration, faces that make for a vibrant painting instead of a wash of one color of paint. We will make a place for them, integrate their past with the future, throw them the lifejackets their elected leaders would say they don't have the budget for. They will not drown. They will see those city lights, brighter than ever.

Something starts to grow around the edges of my vision. I feel it, really, before I notice the faintest shading to the light; a cloud passes slowly until I can make out the shapes. Behind a chain-link fence, a hundred yards back, decorated with razorblades, I make out faces, their eyes outlined with the wire, like bad spectacles sitting as they stare at the spectacle of us, here, in their home.

I want to tell them not to worry, that they are drawn on this map. Our map. *Their* map. They are accounted for and catalogued. They need not fear us. We are bringing the rest of the *world* to them. No longer will they fight for their lives in a ring made of bones. Death will have to find a new haunt, for this patch is his cemetery no longer. The era of the incompetence and ignorance long in effect is over; now, innovation reigns.

>>

My morning is filled with rage. Not my own, I have no righteous indignation - well, perhaps that is an idealistic exaggeration, all our bias shows at times; I should say I have none while at work for I cannot - so the fury is that belonging to you, dear internet commenter. A news story broke last night, rife with divisive issues, as all news stories attempt to be. But some of those stories shatter louder than others, and this is one of them. The noise is deafening, tens of thousands of symbols screaming on one side or other of that dividing line, colliding in a clusterfuck of conjecture and credence. Oh, how you opine!

The thing about the internet and our role in it is, while we do not go so far as to mediate, we must still act as moderators, because unlike conversations in real life, strangers don't step in to stop that first swing from making contact with someone's chin. You think no one has to play peacekeeper, because there is seemingly no threat. No imminent harm to befall. If only that were true. Perhaps one day the scars left on the psyche will be taken as seriously as those left on the skin.

I know you don't read the submission policy or the terms of service before you post anything. I know. It's okay. No one does until they receive that final message informing them they have violated one of those terms and their account has been suspended. Some of them *are* rather arbitrary, I will admit. But everyone should be familiar with the big ones, the kind of speech that is discriminatory and inflammatory, which, at best, is like spray painting the *n-word* or *f*g* or *die c**t* on someone's car, and, at worst, is dragging the blade across their wrists yourself. Would you not expect to be called out if you said such things in a room full of strangers? You would, and so you would stay silent in that situation, keeping those thoughts inside your head where they belong. But here, I am the one calling you out. I am the one telling you to stop talking.

There - there is one. A string of symbols creating a composite of the most hateful, bigoted imagery, slathered in a nice coating of the desire for the death of the different. It is one of those sentences so atrocious it encases you in ice, leaves you chilled and frigid, your muscles contract, everything frozen. You are unable to look anywhere else. The disbelief is thick in the room, I breathe it in like a fog, taste the rank rancor that rises from the most foul place inside a person. Thawing the ice lags; I require so much heat to sink some of the things I see. I take comfort in creating the true north of this compass, though, the navigation, charting a course for seas that are less turbulent than these choppy waters, casting away those passengers that would certainly mutiny, leaving them with a lifejacket upon which is printed the agreements they violated. They can drift awhile, cut off from contact, and reflect on the cold waters numbing their skin.

My watch vibrates and I break contact with the screen for the first time in four hours. There is a tiny icon of ebi fry. As I swipe to clear it another one appears, a bento box, followed by a bowl of ramen and onigiri. I guess Japanese is the general consensus for lunch today. I become aware of the pressure on my bladder and lick my dry mouth. I push away from the monitor and stand, my young joints cracking as though they were old already. I try to stretch them, but realize I don't know much about the wiring of the body, just of the machines. The bathroom line takes about fifteen minutes.

There's a usual group of us that grabs takeout together, trying different places surrounding campus. We meet at the south exit and head towards whatever cuisine is the most adventurous, wanting to experience everything the diversity of this dynamic area offers.

The line at Wabi-Sabi curves around the block, as it usually does on the lunch hour, workers wanting the natto sushi and giant clam shipped in from Japan. We all scroll through the menu on our phones so we can be prepared to order as soon as we get to the counter; it's rude otherwise. Waiting in line well is a social skill required here. Not having made up your mind is a surefire sign of newcomers unacclimated to population density. Usually that slower pace some bring with them is quickly ground out, but a clueless few glide around blithely forever, costing the rest of us our time.

After I place my order I stand against the counter, a thin strip of shelf to place your food while you stand and eat, hoping the *mirugai* will go down easier this time. It's such a popular choice but I can't quite grasp why; I wonder if I just need more ponzu sauce. I must be eating it wrong. Staring across the street, I notice a homeless man sitting on the opposite corner. I feel that same pang in my heart as I do when I hear such hateful words as I did earlier. He must be in such desperate need, his face darkened with dirt, long since abandoned by his family, probably due to mental illness or circumstance beyond his control. I glance to my colleagues to see if they are thinking the same, but they are absorbed in their conversation and I don't want to interrupt. People stream by him, and he just sits, waiting, with his sign.

I scroll through my watch, searching for resources in the area. I see there is a church a few blocks away that gives out free meals to anyone in need. I nudge my colleague to suggest we mention this to the man when we leave. He agrees, and says that he will talk to the man, explain there is a hot meal available to him nearby. He grew up in this city, he is more familiar with what he tells me is called the *street community*, a nicer term for the chronically homeless.

I walk a bit behind the group, lazily twirling the handles of the takeout bag around my fingers, feeling the weight of the food assist oscillation. I see my colleagues up ahead, a collection of kin, tiny bodies holding so many big ideas. One of them pauses at the corner, waiting for the walk signal, and muses to the rest of us if we should give that homeless man one of our old laptops, so he can better access resources. Another laments the lack of free city-wide wi-fi, long since promised but bogged down in bureaucracy. *If only he could see what is out there to help him*, I hear.

If only.

101 five

I am sailing my ship again. I am behind the helm of this barge, forging ahead with the lives of passengers in my hands. So far today the waters are calm but I am alert for a sudden squall, a storm to slam into starboard, breaking the sea legs that are barely steady enough to stand on in this life. I am a sentinel on the quarterdeck for all who choose to travel aboard this vessel, one of thousands in the ocean of information, buying tickets from ports of call to journey distances once thought impossible, hoping to find a land where they feel at home or bring back tales to their own.

We start to approach the breakers, jagged rocks with no lighthouse, no warning, of what you will find among the ruins. A graveyard of nameless young sailors, fragile bodies broken, bones long since drifted down, becoming embedded in coral reefs, gutting fish that mistakenly slide over them. I know there is a sandbar of badness just beneath the surface, and if we are not careful, it can drag along the whole bottom of this ship, leaving us as exposed as the insides of those fish. I look for it, the looming shadow, visible when the sun hits at just the right angle.

And there, blurred by the currents, is one of those shoals, composed of the most dangerous kind of symbols. I see them now, luring the lost towards the beauty promised by the behavior of destruction. If the symbols are to be believed, before long the sailors will want to capsize their personal craft, and the responsibility of righting this wrong falls to me.

There lies a story of the glory of the razor, waxing about wounds as if such a thing could ever be desired, comparing cutting to an orgasm, enticing anyone with easy access to a blade to try this form of release.

I read these beautiful words, an ode to such an ugly subject. This, I am sure, is pure poetry, though it cannot be if it is written as a love letter to *death*! It is too fearful how the rhythm of these words can become a siren's song to call others to cut, a sanguine seduction to come drown in your own blood, exalting the ease with which pain can be removed from the body, as if it were that simple of a solution. Surely, this must be stopped.

Without warning I suspend the account. It is part of our policy to protect people from those that would encourage self-harm of any kind, be it starvation or any other so-called coping strategy that is spread as kindling under a slanderous pyre, piling victims to stoke the sickness. I lean back a bit, satisfied I have done the right thing, both according to my superiors and my own morality.

It is not more than a few moments later that I get a notification on the left of my screen, flashing red, demanding immediate resolution. I see that the user I suspended has filed an appeal to the account termination. I hesitate, pull up the approved responses, copy and paste the first one and reply back. I say if there is anything else I can do to let me know. I start to move away, but there is a gravity to this that pulls me - maybe it was the strength of the words, the weight of them, as if they were an incantation. I glance over my shoulders to the rows of workstations and with a few clicks, find the user's email address and cell phone number from the ticket they submitted and from that, find another profile with chat capabilities.

I know it's not a good idea. But there is some compulsion here, maybe it is the desire to help, to go further, to not see the writer of such beautiful words so infatuated with caliginosity. I see they are online and type the helpline number that appears when users try to view accounts such as this one. I wait, and it is not a moment later that they respond.

I can't say a fucking thing that I want without fear of - You read that didn't you? Just from me tapping? Striking it out makes no fucking difference does it?

Little dots dance on the screen, then stop. They roll out from the ambiguous avatar, then roll back in. I press commands to try to copy that which is not being said but they are too quick and smart and evade capture, striking out the words that cease altogether, and with them so does my breath.

Then it comes, furiously, delivered all at once, this tiny cannonball, aimed for the side of my ship, keyed in elsewhere and then pasted in the chat to eliminate my interference.

You get paid to watch me? How dare you? How do you sleep at night?

I am startled. What do they know of my sleep patterns? No - that is foolish, I am feeling a faint paranoia, probably from my position, from doing what I do every day. But it is a colloquialism, nothing more, the intent of such a phrase a pointed disagreement with my occupation.

I know what I am doing is wrong, and worse still I am doing it badly, letting it affect me. We are not supposed to engage on this level. But their wave of words washed over me; I coughed and spit it all up and have to know what moon is controlling this tide, and if I am strong enough to swim against it. And here, on the rip curl, rides another message in a bottle.

And you say you defend freedom.

I feel the water all around me now. I wait, growing colder. I watch as the lifeboat sinks below the horizon, falling off the edge of the world.

Stay away from me.

Then the last words to me, a string of symbols suspending my body; as I watch this sort of distress signal in semaphore, I fear the flags will hang in my mind as memorial bunting, waving above their mausoleum forever:

What if it was all that I couldn't say that would've saved me?

The ghost follows me around all afternoon. It's like I've adopted a dead pet that I must love and care for in the midst of my routine. And it shits ectoplasm over everything, a milky white reminder of my crimes. Their words, their haunting words, wove me this hairshirt, and I feel their filaments, coarse to their crux, rubbing my skin raw, keeping the pain fresh and at the forefront of my thoughts.

As the end of the day approaches, I try to shrug it off, to leave it at my station along with my failure. I am worthy of a pardon, am I not? Must I be condemned to this incarceration for acting upon my best intentions? But who would bestow upon me that clemency I seek? Certainly not they, the siren, for it is their melody I will hum softly in my cell, slowly going insane from not knowing if their life remains. And there is no monarch to mollify this misery. I will carry the part of me that broke inside this tiny jail, locked away from everyone, so as they never discover the ugliest piece of myself.

I look at the overflow of symbols, all stacked waiting, and realize that they will be here tomorrow, and in the interim more will wash up on the shore.

The shuttle pulls away from campus and I am lulled by the motion of travel, feeling cradled by the familiar seat, two thirds back on the left side. I rest my head against the window and pretend it is a thing of comfort, that I can somehow unmelt the sand in the glass and place my feet in it, transmuting it into a beach. It is thoughts of the spray of the surf cooling my face that takes me away from this day and into sleep.

I wake as the shuttle begins to slow as it exits the carpool lane of the freeway and coasts into its place in surface street traffic, waiting to get through signals. Passengers getting off at the first stop on the outskirts of the city begin to gather their things. This group, I've noticed, is mostly locals or those who came onboard early, before the IPO, who thrive on living where the city screams, while everyone else just wants to be on the edge of where it hums. Their addresses and the coveted local area codes of their cells define them as something *other* than the bulk of us, the transplants.

Blocks are fenced off, with construction

signs hanging from the wire proudly announcing the new projects. I recognize the streets in greater detail after driving my girlfriend here for that site visit. I have overheard mixed reactions to it on the shuttle home, some lamenting the changing face of the neighborhood, while others counteract the cynicism and discuss instead how injecting innovation into the body of this paralyzed community might be the miracle drug to save the longtime residents from wasting.

I can see the stop up ahead, right in the center of the parcel primed for development, which is guaranteed to bring a minimum of five percent (and they say up to twenty) higher rates for renters due to the proximity to our free transit to work. But the shuttle stops short, a block before, the force of applying the brakes suddenly sending devices crashing to the floor. Stunned, I pull the screen up from my window to look, expecting an accident, or anything really, from what is actually out there.

On the street there are barricades, and fabricated plywood coffins, spraypainted with expletives and hate speech I am unable to delete, grenades hurled with pinpoint accuracy to their intended target: us. There is a mob crowded around, carrying banners with fouler language still, telling us - those on the bus - what exactly they think we should do to ourselves. I hear their chants, an invocation of the symbols they have painted on our effigies, trying to bring about our exile from their home.

I feel faint and fearful as I watch them, numb from the shock of uncovering a parallel world that exists next to yours but never touches until they break the barriers. It is like removing sunglasses, your eyes unable to adjust to how bright and sharp the real world is when it's illuminated by the sunlight. Their faces are covered with black bandanas or white masks with mustaches. I can't catch anything of myself, or anyone I know, reflected in their eyes; their hatred makes them something *other*. They start to move towards the bus and I feel myself tense. It's okay, though, there's no way the driver will let them on, and anyway -

My thoughts shatter along with the window next to my head. I watch the spiderweb spread, I see my reflection fragmented and then fall away altogether. Hands grasp at the bottom edge of the windowsill, and start bleeding from the shards - they are trying to climb in! I fall back across the aisle, landing on a colleague, who scrambles out from under me. We all start to push to the front of the bus, but there are more of them at the door pounding on it with bricks. The crush of bodies is immense, it is all we can think about and feel, the heat of each other increasing from the adrenaline of neither being able to fight or fly. When the shuttle starts to rock back and forth, the shouting inside eclipses the sound of sirens in the distance.

I feel the police before I see them, when the

shock of the blast of tear gas canisters enters the crowd. The smoke pours in from the open window and the body that was struggling to hoist itself inside is pulled back. I hear the thump as they land hard on the concrete and see an armored officer put their knee into the suspect's back and zip-tie their hands.

Police swarm now, continuing the barrage of gas and baton attacks, melting the rage of the protesters into puddles as they cry out in agony, too preoccupied now with their pain to be a threat. I watch as their makeshift symbols are smashed by the state, and I am glad for it, I am glad to be protected by those who swear to do so, but as the streets start to settle as they are swept away in vans, I am sad.

I don't understand - without us there wouldn't be documentation of uprisings just like this one all over the world. Our products are banned overseas in countries where the citizens can't use them to express themselves freely like they can here. Why are they targeting us? This isn't right. What have we done?

A coworker nudges me and holds up his phone with the feed coming in. There is a deluge of commentary about the incident already; trying to catch all of it would be like standing under a waterfall with a bucket. He laughs at some of the tags users are assigning, but I am still too anesthetized to find any humor in what happened. I look to the colleagues that live in this neighborhood; they are shaking and muttering as they exit the shuttle, their communication having spun off from the rest of us as soon as the scene quieted. I was hoping to talk to them, to get some insight into the situation, but they didn't seem interested in anyone outside of their circle. My watch keeps vibrating, it is like a blood pressure cuff on my wrist that will keep squeezing until I release everything it wants to tell me. I have messages from my girlfriend and colleagues wanting to know if I am okay and what happened. The whole city will know every minute detail before the nightly news can even make it down here to place someone on the sidewalk and talk. I tell them I am fine; I tell my girlfriend the same and that I will see her tonight.

   A flute is set before me, a familiar shape on a familiar slab of sleek steel, but the color of the liquid inside has changed from a pleasant lavender to a kind of antiseptic blue, set off against the cold gray of the bar.

   "We can't get the old stuff anymore," the bartender sighs. "France stopped exporting it to the US. But this is a nice domestic liqueur, organic, the taste is a bit more floral but we like the color it makes when you mix it with the champagne, a sort of undersea dusk."

   I look over at my girlfriend across the

room and wonder how she will take this news. With a chaser of litigation, perhaps? Negotiating contracts between the US and France, to get that same crème de violette to which she is accustomed. I am fairly certain that *undersea dusk* will not be how she describes the most unpalatable hue her favorite drink has turned.

It is another one of those industry nights that I am floating through, altering the salinity of myself with alcohol to try and remain buoyant. Despite the events of this afternoon, we still attended – or, perhaps, we came *because* of those events. This time, they know I warrant more attention than the crumbs they usually toss my way, as I possess special knowledge that is relevant to them and their aims. I am standing behind a deadline, holding information that separates the success of their project from its failure. I am a survivor, a war correspondent, freshly returned from the frontlines.

But this does not gain me anything with them, not really. News, a democratic essential, is free, and freely I must give it to them. There is no respect to be gained from the exchange, nor any monetary motivation for myself. I tell them what happened because they ask, because it is the truth, it is their right to know what kind of forces conspire against them.

The conversation in the bar is fast and hushed. The worry sags in the spaces between their words. I can read those symbols, though, better than most, the ones they scratch with their silence in the air. To look at them, you would only see a group of well-dressed colleagues out for a bit of fun after work, relaxing after the pressures of managing millions of dollars in development. I see the subtext, and it is fear, and that fear, as fear often does, turns to reactionary measures not based in any best practices or open communication. These are people that are motivated purely by incentives, which in turn limits the scope of their ideas for damage control. I hear talk of giving free laptops to the protesters so they feel included, or letting them come work for a day to see all of the environmental features that are being pioneered in this construction. It isn't the sentiment I mind, it is the baseline of disgust running under it, the exclusionary tone. The flavor of this conversation is as bitter as the old fashioned I sip, perfuming everything acrid, and I am having trouble believing how bad this day tastes.

We are standing around outside the back of the bar, a small group of us that drank straight through to last call and then stayed for one more round while the bartender cleaned up the place. Two of the partners from the firm are leaning against the wall of the alleyway smoking, one a cigarette and one a cigar. I hear the roar of a plane pushing through air and watch red lights on top of buildings blink as signals to stay straight, and think this is one of those perfect city nights, the ones that rub your troubles with the balm of drunkenness. I see her face shimmer with a spark of electricity when she winks at me. I start to relax and hear myself laugh for the first time today.

"Hey - anybody got a cigarette?"

Startled, I turn towards the voice and see a tall man shambling towards us, wearing a tattered overcoat and nearly tripping over his oversized and untied shoes. He is closest to me, so I tell him sorry but I don't smoke. I wait for the partners to do something, to offer him one of theirs, but they stay with their backs against the wall, keeping their eyes on him, cooly exhaling smoke as if it is an abundant resource and they have the sole rights to all of the tobacco plantations. He watches them, and then turns back to me and asks me again if I have a smoke. I tell him sorry, again, and look over my shoulder to the partners, my face aghast at why they aren't stepping in to this awkward conversation.

I start to turn back towards him to apologize for my companions and their lack of manners, and as I am mid-pivot, a wall breaks on my face. I see the fist of the man retracting from my jaw, and then returning again, compounding the blow to obliterate any semblance of fortitude I may have had, and instead sending me off into oblivion.

It is like I have the bends. My body is trying

to equalize to the pressure he exerted, compressing all of the extra dumb space inside me into something just as brutal as he, to continue the beating even as I try to ascend, to hold this ground, to face him. But a last blow is bursting my eardrums and as I slip from standing I am thinking the only way to break through the surface is to swim towards the bottom.

I feel the cold concrete on my back like an unforgiving ocean, and pray to just this once see the stars that are always obscured by smog before I sink into the ground for good. I realize that in this moment, tonight, after a quarter of my life elapsed, this is the first time I've truly come to taste my own blood.

Knowing is like salt in the wound.

Time shrinks, as if something substantial was subtracted between seconds. I see it pass in a kind of lapse, watching the skyscrapers being built in minutes rather than months, a tilt shift of piles of pillars stacked on top of each other by hundreds of hands, glass encasing offices and apartments, gardens growing on rooftops, flowers spilling over the ledge. Parts of the city once familiar are brand new seemingly overnight. How long is it since I accepted this job after college? Months? Years? I couldn't say. My watch could, but I am afraid to look. Am I integral enough to be woven into the fabric of the city, or am I simply absorbed, becoming just another stain? Have I stayed here long enough now to remember a time when this landscape was different? To complain about how things have changed? Have I earned that right? Or can I ever, when I am one of the ones making the changes.

Digits flow in and out of my bank account, but the amount I owe seems to stay stagnant. As the buildings rise so do the prices; everything looks and tastes more expensive. Bonuses barely cover bills, money earmarked for vacations is already spent so I go nowhere. I see photographs of trips my coworkers take, more of my girlfriend with her friends, I see her bags open on the bed as she prepares to leave again. I look back at photos from college and my trips overseas; I suppose I am still paying for the traveling I did.

Each morning the shuttle to work feels more crowded as more jobs are created and filled, the only movement in an immobile economy. Faces flow in from around the world, languages mingle in a beautiful cacophony of multiculturalism, but I can't help but lament my lack. One of them asks me the wi-fi password his first day; I don't know if he notices the dry intonation I use when I tell him it's *MAKEBETTER*. I wonder what they would think of the protests against our little bus, or if they can see the specter of the shattered glass like I can - would it be enough to get them to run out on the visas they came here on? What was it like for them back home, is this nothing in comparison, or is it everything. Will their families recognize their sons after they have been cut and scarred by the malcontented, making their messages heard by any means, leaving etchings across jawlines, reducing industry to rubble.

There is a growing air of discontent, of resentment. It feels like a thin haze has settled over the city, like there is smoke from a fire no one can see burning. The boundaries of the city are dividing lines between those that can afford to live and work here and everyone else. More lines grow around income brackets, thicker ones, defining more clearly the roles.

I duck my head a little more each day when I step on and off the shuttle. I am praying for fall to come faster so I can pull a beanie down over my eyes, or wear a hoodie without looking like a suspect, but this summer continues forever, the sun's illumination disallowing you to hide. It isn't even summer though, not really. Summer is hot and oppressive, this is just *warm*, like the cooling system clicked off one afternoon. The weather is the same every day: 72 degrees and partly cloudy. It is one thing tech does not need to perfect. I know come December it will drop a bit, but never enough for the holidays here to be white and pure. It creates an infinite loop, causing my entire system to become unresponsive. Pleasantness, it seems, is the weather in purgatory.

My joints feel stiffer than usual; I don't understand why this chair isn't giving me the support I need. I hear people talking about standing desks in the new office downtown. Someone suggests I should take one of the free exercise classes, but I am too embarrassed to try; I've never been athletic.

For lunch I wander around the campus from cafe to cafe, searching for that siren in the faces of everyone around me, needing some act of divination, a little miracle like their tears staining the sleeve of someone's Oxford, leaving an imprint of their face. No one ever found out about my transgression, but that doesn't make it okay. I catch myself running my fingers along my collarbone like I am adjusting something I am not wearing. Or maybe I want my nails to become blades and just slit the whole thing wide open.

I catch myself sleeping in places I shouldn't: my desk late in the evenings, on the couches in the breakroom, on the bathroom floor after I get out of the shower. It's like the space I need to exist in is shrinking as everything grows and presses around me. The time I need to be awake is limited to those hours of productivity at work. Maybe it is consideration, trying to take up less as everyone needs more and more. Or maybe it is just exhaustion.

A rare storm has blown in, and with it, my ablution, my baptism. The coming of the torrential rain, the likes of which this city has not seen in decades, is cleansing me of my sins. There is a delicate mist in the hard air blowing in from the west, it is filtering through the fronds of the palms on this Sunday; come tomorrow what is gathering off the coast will break and cause an abatement from our daily lives.

Everything is canceled. School, work, transit - no one is leaving their homes. I am still working from mine, as are many, but this solitude and pause in routine is just what I need. I have the apartment to myself for the week. As they pile sandbags outside, I imagine myself building a barricade around my heart to shelter it from the inevitable erosion of life.

The hypersomnia of late has given way to an insomnia I hope will carry me through the time I have alone. I am productive. I am working more than I ever do in the office. I think I am insulated, here, at home, staring out the windows at the fog covering the buildings below, able to better separate from what I read. A necessary distance has expanded inside me, creating a continent between me and anyone I come in contact with. That perspective I can't explain but was yearning to attain has come alight in me finally. And it may shrink, this new mass, or I will construct bridges, but I needed a little island of my own where I could stand straight. Space is getting so scarce.

I wander around, touching objects I haven't noticed since we moved in and unpacked everything. Or little statues she's brought back from travels I've so far ignored. I finger the glass paperweight, pretending it is a crystal ball and I watch as the clouds that once sat over the future clear, revealing a bright one. The quiet is a blanket I have to throw in the wash, making it my own again, getting rid of her scent. I play all the music she hates and scream along until the neighbors pound on the walls.

This, this is a god damned vacation.

A ping on the computer wakes me. I realize I passed out on the floor working late into the night, and left everything active. Panicked I pull myself up into the desk chair and grab my glasses from where I left them.

The notification, though, is not work. It is personal, college leftovers I never could quite throw out of the relationship fridge no matter how much mold grows, obscuring what was once appetizing. I click accept on the video chat invitation, but tell her I need a minute first and throw on a shirt and muss my hair.

She wants to know how I'm getting along with the weather on the west coast; she, like most everyone back east, is bemused by the reactions and insane preparations. She wants to know if I'll survive it like I did the shuttle attack; it made national news as the epitome of everything that is wrong with the world - pick your side, go ahead, I was just stuck in the literal middle. I don't need to ask her which one she's on, I know better. I tell her the details because she wants them, talking like it's a warm up to a long conversation, instead of a delay to an overdue goodbye.

Because it is always goodbye with us. Regardless of how it starts, it always ends the same way: arguing about the job I took that carried me away from her, and the one she turned down so she could stray further from what were once our shared ideals. And the prelude to our end oscillates between ethics and logistics, and the space between those two is an ugly landscape of disagreement, fraught with obstinance.

That smile of hers that cut me so deeply when we were together now looks like one of sedition; she is forever trying to make me recant against my employ, to turn backwards and accept the anarchism that has come to define her life. The course we charted on the maps of our lives were supposed to take us to the new world together, but she decided to harden up and turn back towards the wind, resigning herself to a lifetime of struggling against the current, thinking it a kind of martyrdom to make daily living as difficult as possible. Instead of making the world better, she wants to unmake it, to embrace entropy.

Everything you pay for is wrong. Anything proprietary is profane, patents impede progress for the people. Buttons on her vest read "capitalism kills," "we are Anonymous," "eat the rich." We both agree existence costs, but she wants it to be free. And I think, in her mind, if she convinces me to defect, it is a victory.

So what is she to me? I suppose it is the same, trying to solve the problem of how someone you love can change so much in the worst way, the way that makes you question your very sanity for ever loving them in the first place.

Love. I did love her, desperately. I consider unlocking my cage and telling her what I have done; a confession. I know of anyone, she would understand why I did what I did. But it will not bring about comfort, it is just further ammunition she will stuff in the barrel and blast me with, peppering my body with the buckshot of my mistake. It must die on those rocks with me.

She notices the shadows of the beating. They still darken my face, follow me around and grow and shrink with the light of the day. She assumes it was from the protest, and that is what I have told everyone else. It happened the same day, the plausibility enabling my denial. But I cannot lie to her.

I tell her the story. It was injury to insult, I joke. I say it was senseless violence that for awhile kept me pacing, searching for answers, meditating on the meaning of a fist to the face. But I came up with nothing, there is no reason; violence is always without purpose.

She says nothing; hesitation is preternatural for her. That means there is so much she wants to say, but dangerous danger if she speaks. I wait in the dark and turn to look at the lights of the bridge outside, glowing in the fog. It's not raining yet, but it will come. The calm before the storm.

Knowing her as I do, there is a storm of her own pounding on the cellar doors of her chest and she is waiting for the single bulb to burn out before she will show me what is concealed by the light.

It comes in questions, as it often does with her. We always argued about her desire to pull out from me that what she wanted me to be, as if she could manipulate it inside of my brain to make it come out my mouth and I'd somehow mean it, though the words were hers alone.

She asks me why I think conciliation and violence are mutually exclusive concepts and I tell her I'm not sure what she wants to hear, but it's kind of like me and her at this point, isn't it? Jointly exhaustive, one of us must always be right until the other is excluded from any possible outcomes from us talking and I don't want to do it anymore. She says okay quickly, but before she turns the camera off, asks me to consider her question and what violence means. I say *nothing* with indignation and listen to the longest sigh leave her I have ever heard, right as the wind picks up outside and starts blowing the city apart.

seven
111

It seems lately the view of that stalwart bridge is the only constant in my life. Scandal has a way of infiltrating every aspect until you come to define yourself by public opinion. You start to see your face as it looks in candid shots coming out of courtrooms, not in front of the bathroom mirror. Of course, my face is only a flash in the background, not the portrait accompanying the headlines. I am behind my girlfriend who is behind the partners of her firm, a figurative feminine presence that is supposed to quell the swell of outrage directed towards the omnipresent old, white men.

I wake up and look at that bridge, try to

count the red taillights I see heading east every morning, a kind of rosary as I pray for another crisis to dwarf the one defining us right now. It is an unfair exchange, one person's pain for another, but what you are willing to tolerate in harsher circumstances is surprising. But, it is not really *pain.* It is enduring an exaggeration, living with libel for awhile, and then rebuilding reputations. It is not the pain of cancer, the pain of lead in your lungs, the pain of watching your child die, compounded by the pain of being unable to afford treatment, magnified by the pain of no one listening to your cries.

I think of the men that died building that bridge. There, at least, is a testament to them, forged in steel that ferries thousands safely across rough waters daily. What of these deaths? What is their legacy but a polluted piece of property so toxic no one will touch it?

The government is going blue holding its breath waiting for someone to come in and save the development, to raise from the dead the skeletons of the buildings promised, to sew them up with flesh and pump blood into the clockwork heart. At some point it will become inevitable, when the immigration reforms industry is pushing pass and visas are tossed like confetti to thousands of skilled workers overseas. And those new employees will not know of this crisis, and move into apartments built on landfill and waste. But if the cleanup were to be done properly, by a company other than the one my girlfriend's firm contracted with, it might not matter.

Until then, we are in a state of hypervigilance. Even though I am only attached peripherally, I mince words, mixing meanings and obfuscating truths like she taught me so well with her forked tongue. It is another relationship where I am tasked with slipping on the skin of another so that we may match while the world watches, and this world, it is always watching. Every hand holding a phone has the potential for the proliferation of imperfections for posterity.

I don't know where I will hang up this suit when it's all over. In another closet, though whose I don't know. Her and I died along with the project. She not only knew what was happening and kept it quiet, but rid the company of the whistleblowers and is now leading litigation against their lawsuit for wrongful termination. There were things hiding inside of her I wasn't equipped to see and this collapse ripped her open to me. I searched her cavities for symbols that would betray her true nature, but found nothing I could read, just a vast absence containing her poverty of morals. I should've known, the need for my presence in her life was never love, only a sluice of goodness she would let flood the gulley of her body when she needed to appear human.

The line we've all been snorting until it makes our noses bleed is that without cost cutting measures, the promised percentage of low-income housing units and new education facilities wouldn't be built, as the dearth of raw materials means the return on that investment is not only a wash but a deficit. It was for the common good to invest in those communities, but without significant government backing, the free resources couldn't be supported by business alone. Tax breaks can't recoup years of lost revenue from below-market-rate rents, especially when the market is a minotaur, destroying the traditional GDP, devouring swaths of jobs relied upon by unskilled and underpaid labor.

So, they say, *so*, I also hear myself saying patently, it's better to have those people in any home they can afford long-term because their factories will shutter in favor of data centers where they will never be able to work. The cleanup of radioactive materials wasn't *botched*, it was done to a degree of affordability so as to make the place livable enough to support these families in structurally-sound homes, while also providing on-site learning centers to encourage their matriculation into the kinds of jobs the future is promising. This was not an intentional act of evil, but one of benevolence, of making a smart investment in this community, in these people. Of making it a better place.

Better. It's a symbol that I keep scratching out in my head so I can see it, but I can't remember the meaning. There are too many voices shouting over this and I can't hear my own anymore. A lot of people lost things when the contract broke, some less obvious than others. For most it was their life or their livelihood. For me it was just the reasons that keep me living.

The shuttle feels like it's a hearse taking me to my own funeral instead of work. I expect it to be a nice open casket affair, the corporeal manifestation of my hopes and dreams laid inside, a wreath hung around the wedding portrait of me and my girlfriend that never happened, our unborn children crying over our lack of love in the front pew. My ghost will give a eulogy to everything I couldn't accomplish for her, noting the deceit she required of me and my easy acquiescence to her will, my silence against the truth speaking so loudly of my character. In my head I pontificate at the pulpit in a way that puts the last few weeks into perspective, but as soon as the bus stops I forget what it was I said that was so edifying.

I pick up my messenger bag and disembark, rubbing my hand over my face feeling for the burst blood vessels I still wear, though faintly. I think that is probably the oldest news surrounding me at this point, bookending the development scandal with the latest personal problem that isn't public yet. I have to add apartment searching to my to-do list, although she is gone on another trip and is letting me stay there, because she is generous and kind, I'm sure. I figure I'll only bother to look down in this area, both to reduce my commute and because I can't afford the city proper on my salary alone.

I push through the glass doors and notice an unusual amount of people milling about in the foyer, the volume of the conversation turned way up. It echos in the open space, the buzz inescapable. I stop walking and refresh the notifications on my watch. The feed is filled with nothing but speculation about the unannounced press conference this morning, with most of the talk focusing on rumors about our founder himself reading the statement. Usually he only speaks when it's about anything game-changing, but we know that everything major in the R&D pipeline is months away from beta testing, so it has to be something unplanned, completely spontaneous - a strategic move, but to what end?

The crowd continues to grow; I don't think anyone is expected to do any work right now. I can't help but start to get a contact high from breathing in all of the excitement everyone is exhaling. And then comes the push, bodies becoming a single organism that moves without being told towards the theatre.

When our founder comes out we usually react like it's a concert and not a work announcement, and this is no exception. If anything, it's louder and more frenetic than ever before, phones in the air to record everything he says even though it's being streamed simultaneously online. He holds up his hands and we quiet before the lights go out. The screen in the theatre flashes with light and then displays an image we have seen passed around in planning meetings that we assumed was decades away from deployment.

What we're looking at is an artistic rendering of lush forest next to the sea, tented with translucent canopies. It is the concept of our future office spaces, a building type the world has never seen: completely transformable, movable structures built in harmony with the surrounding environment for the lowest possible impact. Without needing much foundation and infrastructure, they can go up almost anywhere, almost overnight, and move just as quickly either due to better business opportunities or changes in the environment that make it unsustainable to stay.

With the lights still off and the room completely silent, the image fades into an outline everyone is all too familiar with from the news: the parcels with the stalled development. The aerial view of it starts to dissolve and the first image of the campus concept appears, overlaying the parcel and aligning perfectly with the natural boundaries of the area. One last layer materializes - a date, three months out. The audience loses their minds.

Our founder laughs and thanks us. We listen with rapt attention as he explains that they stepped in to accomplish what government and traditional industry cannot, using this unwanted place for forging ahead with a better kind of building, a better kind of workspace. They are also testing low-cost housing made of the same material, and including a STEM center *inside* the workplace, to better integrate those that are leading now and the youth that will lead tomorrow.

I am in utter disbelief. And then that fades and gives way to joy. I am resurrected after three weeks dead. I am a devout believer at church on Sunday singing hallelujah! I am *saved.* Spread the good word, go forth and multiply, tell everyone: we are doing what no one else could.

I feel vindicated. I ignore the low pang of guilt that says this isn't about me, but secretly I indulge a bit. This is the reason I am *here*, with these people. This is the reason I left my hometown and my college girlfriend to come out to a place where I knew no one, I only knew I wanted so badly for them to indoctrinate me, to baptize me as one of their flock of apostles, diffusing the good word.

Our founder thanks the public for their attention and cuts the live feed. He then continues to address staff, outlining the complete project and the rapid phases crews will progress through to be fully operational in the amount of time it takes the seasons to change (if we had any here). He hints that along with the material design and massive restructuring, there are new policies and products certain key employees will implement from this location; the proximity to government and trade securing advantages this campus lacks. He tells us all to refresh our devices because if you are one of the new leads, you will receive a notification in a few seconds, and then like a drummer about to kick off the concert of the century, counts us down.

Shouts erupt throughout the theatre and I sit and grin at my colleagues, bursting with love and admiration for them and what they will accomplish. They are the prophets the world is waiting for, come to prepare for the messiah. The holy spirit fills them until they speak in tongues, spitting sentences that are both incomprehensible and statements of fact.

A colleague nudges me and points to my watch, silently asking why I didn't synch. I shrug, but he nods encouragingly. Inertly, I tap the symbol and wait the second it takes to refresh.

I was chosen.

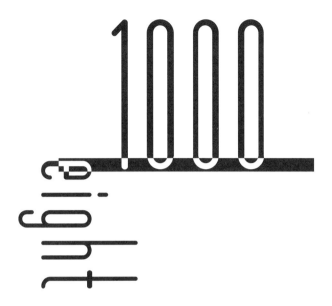

eight1000

There is a dance floor set up underneath the dinosaur. The massive skeletal replica, there more for effect than for authenticity, pulses with different colored lights as smoke snakes around the bones. Alcohol sloshes in cups as couples try to dance, laughing and fizzling more than anything else. The DJ looks intently at the records, never at the bodies, like he doesn't want to know if they really like what he's spinning.

I wander around the museum during one of their adult-only nights. We were given free passes at work and my lunch group decided to go, but at this point I've lost them all despite getting notifications of their locations on my watch as they move from room to room. I'm enjoying the solitude, though, standing on the transparent bridges over illuminated pools, staring at the stingrays skulking underneath my feet, twisting away as sharks float in.

An albino alligator is sunken beneath the first level, sharing the enclosure with unconcerned turtles. We all lean over the railings like fools, hoping to get closer to him. I'm waiting for someone to lose a flagship phone to the pit when they stretch to take a photo, but it doesn't happen, at least on this visit. I give up and meander through the rainforest, a multi-level domed ecosystem that is able to support birds living far from their tropical homes. It is perhaps the best aviary you'll find anywhere.

Plenty of women are here in small groups but I don't approach any of them. I'm a decent dancer, but I'm too afraid to start alone and wait until someone joins me. Not here, this is ultimately a temple of knowledge, not a bar. Something about it seems sacred, in a strange way.

Instead, I step out onto the roof. It is a moonscape made of moss, a breathing organism, designed to support native plants. The water from the aquarium recycles through here, creating a self-sustaining permaculture perfect for living with limited space and resources. Elements invented for this building will be incorporated into ours.

Shrieks come from the foliage, and I see flashes of flesh as bodies are rid of their clothing, the youth of the city experiencing being alive. The night is clear and cold, a few layers of fog nestle the trees in the distance. I'm not sure if exhibitionism was what the museum was hoping to exhibit to raise more money for the always-struggling institution with events like this, but it's a start, and it's a story, and that might do well enough for them.

I feel a thud of arms around my shoulder, jostling me in a friendly manner, and I am hit with the scent of weed mingling with tobacco.

"One day this will be the whole world." He points to the parking lot laid out before us. There are thousands of cards and more museums beyond that, filled with art, sculpture, history, science.

"Just silos of knowledge between dead spaces and deserts."

I twist my head and look at him, his bowtie is askew and his vest unbuttoned, the spliff dangling from his lips. I ask him if he's taking a break, and he laughs, and I feel as if I've missed something that passed between us I couldn't see in the dark. He takes a step away from me, no longer touching, but stays nearby, puffing rings, smoke signals, ephemeral symbols belonging to a meaning of his own I can't discern.

We face away from the crowd and look at nothing together. I want to ask him something, but he is stoic in a way I am not used to seeing. There is a sort of kinship between us, though; I feel like I know him from somewhere I've forgotten belonging to, and I want him to help me remember.

"This is my second job, you know," he says and turns towards me. I start to stutter and he cuts me off.

"Save it. I know how you types are. Always have to be nice to the help, lest it be *inferred* y'all are anything else." He pauses, runs his hand across his jaw and leaves it there. He speaks quietly.

"I'm a technical writer for the largest private energy company in the state. Hell, on the whole west coast. But even that shit ain't making enough for rent anymore. *With* seven fucking roommates in the flat sharing bunk beds. I bartended in college for extra money." He flicks the spliff off the roof, buttons his vest and re-ties the bow around his neck.

"And it looks like I still do." He gives me a slight bow I can only assume is sarcastic as he tells me to enjoy the rest of the party. I watch him walk across the roof until he disappears at the stairs; his absence makes me feel like I should make it easier on him and throw myself through the skylight, impaling myself on the counterfeit fossils.

I doubt I could aim well enough to hit the tip jar on the way down.

Every night now the streets leading onto the freeway are filled with people with signs on both sides. They are in direct opposition and the rest of us, the undecided, drift between them. It isn't that I haven't made up my mind on the measures, just that I don't feel strongly enough to advocate for or against them. And, I try to remain neutral unless it directly affects my work and we take a position. Cars stuck at red lights either honk in support or the drivers yell in frustration.

They flow from the sides of the streets straight to the corners. There is a person with a clipboard stationed on every one, gathering signatures, registering voters, selling buttons. Strangers stop to argue with the volunteers, mostly the elderly or college students, the demographics with the most free time to be involved. Laptops set up on the tables show documentaries or propaganda pieces, it's the same either way, really, you just call it one or the other if you agree with the message.

This election season is more contentious than usual. There are a number of controversial ballot initiatives, some involving amendments to the state constitution. Money flows in from other states trying to influence the outcome, for fear whatever takes hold here may spread. We are the great innovation incubator to the rest of the country, trying things here never thought of elsewhere. When they work, they are adopted widely and we are praised, but when they don't, those that never took the chance are quick to explain where exactly it went wrong and how they would never make such obvious mistakes.

For me, it's all about cleaning up the mud getting slung right now. There are fields of it, everyone is knee-deep in manure with shovels in hand, digging up any dirt they can on the opposition and aiming between the eyes. It is a vulgar business, getting what you want, when what you want either adds to or removes from the quality of life of those different from you. If people were to tilt their head slightly and alter their orientation, they might find the parallels between them and those they fight against. But instead they toe their party lines even after the bottles are empty and everyone else has passed out on the couch or gone home.

I head into work. I walk confidently off the shuttle now, knowing my time here is coming to a close as soon as the rapid construction finishes. Those of us that are going to the new campus are given a bit more reverence now, though it is silly to think I am somehow more qualified than anyone I work with. You don't get hired by this company if you aren't dedicated. But, I am excited, both for the extra responsibilities and to be one of the test subjects of working in a building that is capable of conforming to change, to adapting to our input. Improvements will no longer require waiting for another office, they will be made in real time. I shiver a bit every time I think of it.

I don't even make it to my desk before my watch pings with an urgent alert. I am being summoned, not by my supervisor, but the department head. I assume it's in regards to the move, though I know we have meetings scheduled to discuss the transition. I run up an extra two flights of stairs and wait in the small lounge outside his office until his assistant opens the door for me.

He is not alone, but the other people in the room clearly do not work here. They are too formal, dressed far nicer than even our executives do during a press conference. Little pins sit on their lapels, denoting their political affiliations. I noticed they are in fact mixed, something I was not expecting. Behind them, close to the wall, are law enforcement officers - I don't know if they are city police or something more specialized.

They shake my hand and introduce themselves, and I vaguely recall voting for one of them a few years ago, my first election here, I think. We chat about restaurants nearby and where they are going to lunch later and what the drive was like, and I am struck by how much time we are wasting. No one here begins a business conversation with niceties. We save them for the bars after.

An hour later I understand what they want and what I am to do, and there is a great unease growing in me. I am to switch from clearing only content flagged by other users, my sole job since I started, to monitoring specific accounts that target these individuals and their cohorts, many of whom are up for re-election and are finding it difficult to interact appropriately with all the new forms of technology. Campaigning, they tell me, has changed a lot since they started. Offices are no longer filled with the best baby kisser, but belong to those who master communicating online. And when mistakes are made, they are immutable.

It's now my job to change that.

I try not to think about it too much. It is only temporary, until ballots are cast and I move to my new position. The experience, they say, is the perfect compliment to what I will be doing in the new office. I sift through user after user, connecting similarities and compiling profiles, some of which, if they are too incendiary, I turn over to the authorities as I was directed, to be entered in a database, so they might better fight domestic terrorism.

Mostly though I just delete that which they sought to preserve. An elected official or hopeful candidate makes an unpopular, ignorant comment (denoted by an "ist") and someone captures it before it's deleted. They then post it elsewhere, to preserve a record, to combat the defense of hypocritical deflection. I go and delete *that*, so that everyone might get a fresh start. The idea being it is the original user's right to expunge their own speech.

I am starting to feel like little more than a redactor, inking the internet with a big black pen.

A diversity of symbols replaced with one, that thick line you can't see anything behind.

I think of my faith in this company, and what we do, and get stuck on this incongruence. For the first time I find myself asking what the priest hides under his robes. What he meditates on before he speaks. Is it god and how we best serve him? Or is it how he might better serve himself? I thought I was here to facilitate dialog, to remove the barriers long considered impediments to free speech. This is a time when we are tasked with deciding who to best represent us on critical issues, and this was supposed to be the medium wherein anyone could reach those historically-isolated few, to hold them accountable, to demand better, to make our voices heard. But if they won't answer, what use is it?

A one-way conversation is not a conversation. It is a sermon.

1001 mine

Near the edge of the city sits a citadel, a bastion of innovation, untouched by the rules governing the rest of the country. This fiefdom is an entirely deregulated living laboratory, without the antiquated laws that have strangled advancements and delayed reforms in the discipline that ultimately determines our survival. It is a chance to finally see what we are capable of. In our little feudal system, one ascends to the throne not from lineage but by brains and imagination.

This place is also a safety valve. The surge that will spill forth from our minds will not always contain pure liquid. The sludge that will surely collect needs to pass through a sieve before it is suitable for public consumption. Instead of requiring permission to move forward with each stage of a project that might end up insignificant and wasteful, we can try them on our own terms and then adapt them to the requirements of a particular jurisdiction after they have proven successful.

We are already operating at a loss, though, a moral bankruptcy. The company did manage to properly remove radioactive contaminants from the land in exchange for the exemption from governmental interference, in a sort of hushed backroom usurping, pointing to the lack of ability on their end and the wealth of it on ours. But the removal massively altered the area, taking out truckloads of dirt as the water rushed back over to cover what was once space built of bayfill. That in turn eliminated space for the planned low-income housing units. All we did was collect the dirt and shovel it onto this neighborhood that's had one foot in the grave for a century.

Housing is desperately needed all over the city. I may work in the dazzling addition to the skyline, but I live in a closet.

It's all there is. It is all that is left in this city. We are far beyond maximum operating capacity. People, more and more of them, were gathering outside the limits, waiting to push through. And then there were enough of them to form a critical mass, their bodies streaming into the city, passing through solid objects to embed themselves in any open space they could find.

I hung around my ex's apartment for way too long, dragging my feet on making a decision about moving, unwilling to become roommates with anyone from work. When the new office opened, an influx came from the south and those of us that waited found ourselves renting receptacles instead of rooms. You may think I exaggerate when I say closet, but I assure you, it is a literal closet. My rent is a little less than what I paid with my old girlfriend, and I make a little more with the promotion. I don't have to wake up early for the shuttle, so I can get coffee out most mornings. It's not a bad deal, really. So long as I never try to do anything other than sleep and shower there.

I moved in election night. The TV and computers in the rooms of the loft were streaming numbers and percentages as the results rolled in. They were mixed; neither party blew enough hot air to ignite the flames inside everyone, but an initiative was able to amend the state constitution in order to remove basic human rights from certain types of people. Lawyers started preparing appeals the minute after the measure was called. I'd like to think *she* was working on it, but I know better. She probably helped draft the language of that damn bill in the first place.

Anger poured out after the election, a black ooze from every orifice of the public, from both the winners and losers. Flippant comments became cause for the end of careers. Strongly-worded posts were shared with ferocity, calls were made to employers and school administrators demanding those that dared disagree be ostracized, that they wear little letters of their crime forever. Symbols stitched to their shirts, denoting their singular stroke against the prevailing ideology.

Opinion pieces by authors and professors criticizing this practice were removed from websites, and anywhere that re-posted them was shut down as well. Sites and accounts originally started as muckraking entities hit the delete button on themselves to avoid the kind of lashing they watched their peers take, even those on the other side of the aisle from them. Information, I fear, is cascading away from accessibility. Worse still, the loudest accusers had the least amount of credentials to substantiate their claims, yet this emerging culture of deletion helped deflect that for them, while forty-year careers were forced to end in resignation.

They promised me I could develop programs with my own team once I moved here, and that one they honored. So I try to keep things alive that enmity would see dead. To place blankets over them before they freeze to death from the chill. It feels like the only good work left. I will never invent anything, I was not made for that. But maybe I can preserve things. I think of what might be said that saves someone one day, what unexpected heat source will warm that person on the precipice of slipping away. I think maybe in my work here I am turning into little more than a caveman sitting around a fire, but it is only because I feel how cold the world is becoming.

Usually after work I stop at a cafe on the way home for dinner, sometimes taking transit to a farther one out on the ocean, where I can watch it break on the beach at high tide; but most nights it's the one between work and my living space ("home" seems a cruel thing to say, doesn't it?). I'll grab a sandwich or salad and go a few more blocks to a small, decrepit park, full of rickety playground equipment and dogs roaming free of their owners. It is quaint in that miserable way of being something that is yet to be improved.

The same kids play soccer here almost every night. I sit on a bench in the park across from my rental unit and watch them while I eat, trying not to seem like a threat, like the weird lonely man that I am. It's just that it is like a meditation, the movement of young bodies whizzing past each other, a ball flying in the air, shouts and laughs and shit talking, the brief escape of problems and differences so long as the game is going.

I finish my food and stand to go to the garbage when I see a few guys from work saunter up, dressed for soccer in knee high socks and spiffy little matching sponsored jerseys plastered with the logo from a start-up we acquired recently. They head to the benches and put their duffel bags down and wait, the sun starting to slip away. The kids, still running around in their old t-shirts and backwards caps, don't seem to notice. The lights click on, emitting their electric drone. After more of my colleagues gather, one of them approaches the kids in the middle of the field and starts talking to them.

I toss my container and walk closer to the chain link fence separating the field from the rest of the park, but I can't tell what's going on. All of the kids have stopped playing at this point, though, and are gathering around the conversation between their friend and my coworker. Most of them aren't even old enough to drive, only reaching up to the chests of the newcomers.

As the intensity of the conversation increases, their voices raise enough for me to make out the gist of what they're saying - they paid to reserve the park tonight for a match, but for the kids, this place has always been free and first-come, first-serve. I see a white piece of paper waving in the childrens' faces. The youngest start dispersing, but a few of the older ones hold their ground and ask if they can all make new teams and play together. Some of the men agree and start to shake hands, but the one with the permit steps inbetween, holding it high, displaying it as an intractable decree.

I tap in the name of the park on my watch and search for news sorted by most recent, and immediately understand what's happening.

Unable to scrape together enough revenue to make the necessary repairs, the city started offering a paid reservation system to try to generate the funds to fix the park. But those that have always relied on the park as a free place to go after school can't afford the permit. They say this pay-to-play system is needed to revitalize communal resources all over the state, but it is not a welcome change to long-time residents, and often creates a barrier to access for those that need it most.

As they exit, the kids pass by me and I hear their frustration towards the breakdown of a system they relied on for the entirety of their short lives. They are angry that *their* park was co-opted by men they've never seen, who moved here from places they've never heard of, who were able to take away a piece of their hometown only because of their ability to navigate a system none of them even knew existed. Nothing is stable for them after this; I can see it on their faces, hear it in their cries.

That's the thing about everybody in the pool: someone will always be displaced.

I stare at the dowels above me where my

clothes hang, an awful grown-up version of a mobile, made of polos and khakis. I must admit I miss the view of the bridge I had with my ex, and feel like a privileged asshole about it, and then wonder how a privileged asshole came to live in a closet.

What am I actually doing here?

I think about leaving, but it would be like choosing to step out of the future to stay in the past.

The door to the room swings open and one of my flatmates sticks his head in, holding up a six-pack.

"Get out of your fucking closet and stop being emo, man."

I know when he's in one of these gregarious moods there is no stopping him, so I oblige.

"Dude, we have the house to ourselves for a week! We need to find chicks and fuck them in these assholes' beds while we can. All those idiots are going to party in the desert where they'll get dehydrated and die, hopefully."

Being the poorest residents of the house, we share a secret bitterness towards the rest of them that made it through school without student loans.

"What are they doing out there?"

He shrugs.

"You know, that crap they do every year. Get wasted and then burn down a giant sculpture it took an artist months to make."

"Why?"

"I suppose to see how fast something

someone else built can be destroyed."

He opens the beer bottle with his teeth and takes a swig. "Better than your own creation, right?"

"Yeah?"

"Yeah."

He slaps me on the back and hands me a beer he forgets I can't open without a tool. I pull my keys out of my pocket and pop the top off in the time it takes him to finish his first one. He slams it down on the dresser and looks at the massive bedroom where he's never been able to afford to sleep.

"What a bunch of cunts."

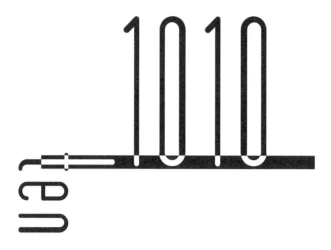

neon 1010

I wander around the streets alone most nights, exploring different neighborhoods. I spend as little time in the closet as I can, unsurprising, I know, stifling as it is, especially on those nights when my roommate asks to shut the doors on me for privacy. This is a joke, right? This is what college bought me. It's the god damned scam of the century.

Chinatown is all neon with symbols I can't translate. It's relaxing, not knowing what they say. I really don't want to know the etymology of their lines and circles. I stare at the roasted ducks as they rotate in the windows, pass by the fortune cookie factory, see all the cheap electronics manufactured overseas spread out on tables for tourists. Sometimes I'll grab takeout and think back to the place I used to go near my old campus, and why I felt the need to eat the house special. Is being offensive the worst thing we can do?

I look to the water and imagine it as it was a hundred years ago, with immigrants streaming in on junks, irregular sails convex as they pulled into harbor. Those wooden pillars are mostly gone, the rotted tops of some pylons extending above the waterline when the tide runs out, temporarily exposing what time buried. I adjust my sails to ensure I keep drifting in the doldrums.

I leave Chinatown through the front gates and wait for the bus back to my part of town, food in hand, in one of those iconic pink plastic bags no one can seem to ban from their restaurants and shops despite paper replacing them everywhere else.

The city bus pulls up and I scan my work ID, which means I always ride free since we heavily subsidize all transit now in exchange for using the stops; a deal worked out to assuage the protesters and for positive publicity. I grab one of the only seats I see, right at the front, an elderly woman pressed into my shoulder on one side, the thighs of young men standing and holding onto the straps on the other. All the different languages mingle; I don't know how many of them know English. There was a time when it wasn't necessary to know it to live here. What words in our language do they know? The name of my company? The products we make? Do they care? Have I ever touched a single life I now sit with? Do they want things to make their lives easier, to connect them with each other, or do they just want to get through life? And I can't even ask, because I never bothered to learn how to talk to them. Maybe if I could just get them laptops...

The bus glides to my stop and I leave and head towards the same bench in the park. Most of it is closed right now for renovations, the permits paying off, but after the construction workers go home, the kids come back and hop the fence to play soccer underneath the streetlights. I try to catch part of the game, just to know that they're fighting their own kind of fight, shadowboxing injustice in the night.

There's already someone sitting there, smoking. He's sitting all the way to one side, though, leaving room for someone else, so I sit and ask if he minds. He shrugs and says it's cool. I ask him if he wants any of my food, and he turns to me with his whole body, to face me straight on, like he needs to confront the kind of question I'm asking him.

But he says nothing, just sizes me up and puffs away at his cigarette, until the gathering of the kids, yelling in the way only youth can, breaks the silence sitting between us like a third person.

I finish my fried rice and toss the paper container in the compost, although I know no matter how quickly it breaks down, it will still outlast me at this point. I hear the click of a lighter and look back to the man on the bench, who is lighting up a joint. The fresh crisp scent of weed mixes with the lingering nicotine, and it takes me back to a night when I dropped a moment and watched it break in front of me.

"Hey, hey I know you!"

He looks up at me with more suspicion than when I offered him food. I point to myself.

"From here? From the museum, I mean? On the roof?"

"Man, you ain't *from* here." He inhales. "But I already knew that." He nods and gestures to the bench. I resume my seat and he passes me the joint.

"Did you grow up here?" I ask him as I take a drag and cough a little.

"Naw, I grew up in the 'burbs, south of here. And this was the dream, living in the big city. Every kid on a fucking cul-de-sac wanted this life." He leans his head back at looks at the quickly darkening sky, clouded over. You can't ever see the stars.

"And now I've got it." He looks back to me with fresh eyes, sizes me up again. I don't mind.

"How are you doing for yourself out here?"

I hold out my hand towards him, index finger and thumb pinched together, asking for another hit.

"Me? Oh, great. I live in a closet now."

He laughs, and pauses, and watches my face. "No shit?"

"No shit."

He laughs harder.

"That's beautiful, truly. Did you get laid

off? Or are you thinking you're gonna make it big, all entrepreneur-like with your own start up?"

"Worse, almost. I got a promotion." I tell him the building I work in and watch him react the same way everyone does. No one is immune. "I just have a shitload of student loans. Couldn't afford college otherwise, and I thought with the field I was going into -"

He keeps laughing, warmly now.

"We *all* thought that five years ago." He runs his finger along an imaginary timeline in front of him. "'With the field we're going in to....'"

He swipes saliva off his tongue and puts out the cherry on the joint.

"How is it working there, anyway? I mean I've toured the building, because my work wants to do the same thing now - of course - but I mean the company, are they as good to work for as everyone says they are?"

"Yeah -" I start, and then hesitate. "I mean, I'm pretty lucky, right?"

He nods. "Sure you are. Lucky as fifty thousand other people. Luckier than fifty million."

I nod along with him. I feel a tug and catch his gaze. He leans forward, hands on his knees.

"But you can be lucky and not happy, right?"

A loud, severe noise explodes somewhere near us and resonates, touching us with vibrations. We don't flinch, just keep sitting on the bench, looking at each other, and in that moment, I know I am a part of this city.

"Gunshot?" I ask.

"Nah... mmm... maybe." He cocks his head. "I don't know, that sounded longer than a gunshot to me. And there was only one. There's hardly ever just one."

We wait a few seconds, but nothing follows.

"Usually there's only one if they shoot an animal," I offer.

"Of course, *that* depends on the definition."

I tap my watch instinctively to look for notifications or alerts and he whacks me in the arm.

"You'll find out tomorrow, man. Or not."

I want to offer a counterargument but I can't really; he's right. I hear the soft pop of the kids kicking the ball into the air, quieted by the din left in my ears from the noise.

"Remember back when *my* fucking company's negligence blew up that pipeline and killed all those people and then everyone had to pay them back for it with service rate increases? That sound, *that* was like thunder gone wrong. I'll never forget it."

"I ... didn't live here then."

He nods. "No, of course you didn't."

"We have photos of the clean up though, at work, or at the old campus," I rush to add. "Our company donated tons of staff time and experimental mapping technology to help locate bodies quickly in case there were any survivors."

"That's great man, really great. Don't bring back the eight that died. Don't lower utility prices. Don't hold anyone responsible. Don't do much else other than showing the rest of us what you can do that we can't. Makes you useful, though. Makes you the *makers*."

I am kind of incensed for the first time tonight.

"Yeah I know, we're all fucking evil, right?"

He leans back, away from me.

"I didn't say that. I *know* my company's worse. We don't do half the charity shit yours does. You don't cut off people's power and let them live like peasants in the dark. We're the evil ones. Or, one of many, I guess."

"Well, what are we supposed to do about it, then? Should I quit? Would that make it better? Move back home to the Midwest and dig for potatoes in the dirt?"

"I mean, you could. That wouldn't stop the machine, though, would it? Just take you out of it. You, my friend, are standing on the right side of history." He chuckles. "The white side. Do yourself a favor and enjoy it."

He stands and extends his hand, and we shake. I watch him walk off towards the kids and he starts running around with them, high-fiving and offering to play goalie. They cheer when he lets a shot go through, and boo when he catches the ball. He doesn't stop smiling.

I look back one last time at his confident, strong face, knowing I'll probably never see him again. It isn't that often you make friends in this city, and it's rarer still to run into them.

The next morning I am late for work for the first time since I started. And not just by a few minutes, but several hours. I am *spectacularly* late. I sent in the appropriate messages and shower and drink all of the coffee in the house to try to clear the fuzz from my head. I am not used to marijuana. I've got a little time to kill though since I said I'd be in after lunch. The apartment is empty so I pad around, naked and wet from the shower, for the first time since I moved in. I walk to the window and stare at the cement wall of the building five feet away from this one. It is gray. And unfeeling. It is not the majesty of the bridge. It is not even the charm of the derelict park. It is a slab of drab concrete.

I sigh and get dressed, a little nicer than usual since I said I was at a last-minute appointment, tucking a dress shirt into slacks, and decide to call a car service and do a few errands downtown.

I step out of the car in the financial district, the home of the venture capitalists that cough up all the money for our ideas. Not negotiating those deals I don't spend a lot of time here, but I wanted to see about some loans to purchase a condo if I can. How many more years will I add to my debt in order to get out of that closet? What's longer than a life sentence?

It's a bit before when we'd break for lunch at my work, but this part of the city still runs on the ancient banker time, where they come and go at precise, brief intervals, disappearing before the rest of us are able to leave work. We can either conform to their schedule or exist without money.

The doors, done in gold filigree a hundred years ago, open and expel all of the essential staff. I am startled by how young most of them are; I suppose I still have my own old ideas of what bankers look like. I blend in with them since I'm dressed up and fall in step, walking wherever they are headed.

They fill up the cafes and restaurants and corner sandwich shops. The type of food doesn't seem to be of any importance to them, there is not a diversity of cuisine here, what matters is the speed and efficiency. But as for their aesthetics, they remind me of my lunch group at the old campus. The three requisite ethnicities, short haircuts styled with gel, thick silver watches or the latest in gadgets adorning their thin wrists - they are me and I am them. I queue up and order food since I haven't eaten since last night and I figure the banks are empty of their primary lenders anyway right now. They talk amongst themselves and I am left to observation.

You know how when everything is what

you're used to seeing you can't really notice what's missing? This scene is so much a reflection of my own, I take what's in the frame as all there is, forgetting that without a wall, there is nowhere to hang the mirror.

There is a stunning lack of women. Once I am aware of their absence, that void is all I can see. It is nearly all men. I think back to my company, which prides itself on hiring a diverse staff, including sponsoring qualified candidates from other countries, yet the vast majority are male. I don't think my ex-girlfriend's law firm was even this poorly skewed towards my gender.

And it comes to me suddenly, like that fist in the face, the perspective I needed but couldn't engineer. Drawing those lines that lead from the front of the canvas to the back, creating a continual view of the past and the present, connecting it all together to point towards the future.

We are not special, or unique. We are like any other time in history: a small group of elite men influence, build and create that which dictates the lives of everyone else, and they go along accordingly, not necessarily because they want to, but because they must, because their voices aren't represented in the dialog. There isn't anything inherently noble or pious or rebellious in what I am doing every day. What any of us are doing every day.

We aren't making the world a better place. We are just making the world.

ABOUT THE AUTHOR

K.I. Hope is the author of two other novels, *hector* and *This is Not a Flophouse*. Her non-fiction reporting appears in various places online and in print; her creative prose is in several anthologies.

She wrote the entirety of this book on a laptop.

Hope graduated from San Francisco State University in 2009; it cost her a lot to say that.

She likes cold nights, coffee, marshmallows, October, rain & sparkly lights; and dislikes people she knows, distances & the chilling effect.